Dear Parent:

Congratulations! Your child is taking the first steps on an exciting journey. The destination? Independent reading!

STEP INTO READING® will help your child get there. The program offers books at five levels that accompany children from their first attempts at reading to reading success. Each step includes fun stories, fiction and nonfiction, and colorful art. There are also Step into Reading Sticker Books, Step into Reading Math Readers, Step into Reading Write-In Readers, Step into Reading Phonics Readers, and Step into Reading Phonics First Steps! Boxed Sets—a complete literacy program with something to interest every child.

Learning to Read, Step by Step!

Ready to Read Preschool–Kindergarten
• big type and easy words • rhyme and rhythm • picture clues
For children who know the alphabet and are eager to begin reading.

Reading with Help Preschool–Grade 1
• basic vocabulary • short sentences • simple stories
For children who recognize familiar words and sound out new words with help.

Reading on Your Own Grades 1–3
• engaging characters • easy-to-follow plots • popular topics
For children who are ready to read on their own.

Reading Paragraphs Grades 2–3
• challenging vocabulary • short paragraphs • exciting stories
For newly independent readers who read simple sentences with confidence.

Ready for Chapters Grades 2–4
• chapters • longer paragraphs • full-color art
For children who want to take the plunge into chapter books but still like colorful pictures.

STEP INTO READING® is designed to give every child a successful reading experience. The grade levels are only guides. Children can progress through the steps at their own speed, developing confidence in their reading, no matter what their grade.

Remember, a lifetime love of reading starts with a single step!

www.randomhouse.com/kids

www.stepintoreading.com

Educators and librarians, for a variety of teaching tools, visit us at
www.randomhouse.com/teachers

Library of Congress Cataloging-in-Publication Data
Landolf, Diane Wright.
Sammy's bumpy ride / by Diane Wright Landolf.
    p.   cm.   — (Step into reading. A step 1 book)
SUMMARY: Sammy and the Koala Brothers help build a train track.
ISBN 0-375-83056-1 (pbk.) — ISBN 0-375-93056-6 (lib. bdg.)
[1. Railroads—Trains—Fiction.   2. Koala—Fiction.   3. Australia—Fiction.]
I. Title.   II. Series: Step into reading. Step 1.
PZ7.L2317345 Sam 2005   [E]—dc22   2004010458
Printed in the United States of America   10 9 8 7 6 5 4 3 2 1
STEP INTO READING, RANDOM HOUSE, and the Random House colophon are registered trademarks of Random House, Inc.

Sammy's Bumpy Ride

Adapted by **Diane Wright Landolf**
Based on the TV series *The Koala Brothers*
Illustrated by **Tom Brannon**

Random House 🏠 New York

Sammy drives his truck.

He takes a shortcut.

It is a bumpy ride.
Sammy likes it!

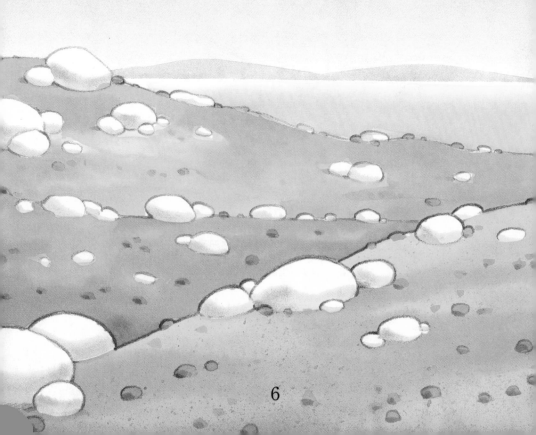

Bang!

What did Sammy hit?

It is a train track!

He wants a train ride.

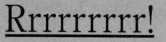

Rrrrrrrr!

Sammy hears a sound.

He looks up.

Sammy waves.

It's the Koala Brothers!

Sammy shows
his friends
the train track.

They all wait
for the train.

But no train comes.

The track is too short.

"We can help!"
says Frank.

Frank and Buster
help Sammy build
more track.

The three friends
pound the spikes.

Now the track
goes right into town!

Will Sammy get a ride?

He waits.

The train still
does not come.

Frank has an idea.

They can ride
the track car!

The friends climb on.
Sammy and Buster
pump the handle.

They go fast.

It is a bumpy ride!

Sammy likes it!

Sammy likes

the bumpy end, too!